THE BIONIC BANANA

More fun from the creators
of *The Bionic Banana*—
The Six-Million-Dollar Cucumber
(available in a Laurel-Leaf edition)

LAUREL–LEAF BOOKS bring together under a
single imprint outstanding works of fiction and
nonfiction particularly suitable for young adult
readers, both in and out of the classroom.
Charles F. Reasoner, Professor of Elementary
Education, New York University, is consultant
to this series.

THE BIONIC BANANA

E. RICHARD AND
LINDA R. CHURCHILL

PICTURES BY
CAROL NICKLAUS

LAUREL-LEAF BOOKS

Published by
Dell Publishing Co., Inc.
1 Dag Hammarskjold Plaza
New York, New York 10017

Text copyright © 1979
by E. Richard Churchill
and Linda R. Churchill

Illustrations copyright © 1979
by Carol Nicklaus

Laurel-Leaf Library ® TM 766734,
Dell Publishing Co., Inc.

ISBN: 0-440-90852-3

RL: 4.9

Reprinted by arrangement
with Franklin Watts, Inc.

Printed in the
United States of America

First Laurel-Leaf printing—July 1981
Third Laurel-Leaf printing—October 1981

Contents

By the Bunch

What's yellow, unbelievably strong,
and costly beyond imagination?

A bunch of bionic bananas.

●

How did Mother Banana spoil Junior?

By leaving him out in
the sun too long.

●

Where should a
twenty-four-pound banana go?

On a diet.

●

How can you tell a
banana from an aspirin?

Bananas come in bunches.

●

What can be washed in warm water,
dries quickly, and needs no ironing?

A drip-dry banana.

A banana swallowed an entire window,
which caught in its throat.
Why did the banana complain?

> It had a pane in the neck.

•

What do you call a
banana who is in prison?

> A convict.

•

Did the police capture
the shoplifting banana?

> No, the banana split.

•

Why don't bananas ever
get beaten up or mugged?

> They usually hang around with
> a bunch of their friends.

•

What's yellow and goes
click, click, click?

> A ball-point banana.

What did the handsome boy banana
say to the pretty girl banana?

"You appeal to me."

●

When is a rotten banana
at its artistic best?

When it draws flies.

●

Who wears a cape and fights crime?

Superbanana.

●

Which early explorer wrote
about his trip to China?

Marco Banana.

●

Who is yellow and
fights forest fires?

Smokey the Banana.

●

What is yellow and hums?

An electric banana.

Why don't bananas have dandruff?

Did you ever see a
banana with hair?

•

Why don't bananas worry when
people say bad things about them?

Bananas are noted for
their thick skins.

•

Have you ever seen
weather stripping?

No, but I saw a banana peel.

•

What do you call a banana
who attends school?

A student.

•

Who costs a fortune to repair,
works for the OSI, is yellow,
and has her own TV program?

The Bionic Banana.

An Apple a Day

If an apple a day keeps the doctor
away, what does a garlic clove do?

Keeps everybody away.

•

What does an apple's aunt look like?

Not a whole lot different
from an apple's uncle.

•

When are apples most like books?

When they are red (read).

•

Why didn't the apple tree
raise young pears?

It couldn't bear them.

•

What's red and has teeth?

An apple. (I lied
about the teeth.)

Why don't apples visit
the dentist twice a year?

> We just told you,
> apples don't have teeth.

•

Why don't apples have teeth?

> Because they don't have
> any fingernails to bite.

•

What did the apple say
to the hungry worm?

> "You're boring me."

•

Why did George Washington
chop down the cherry tree?

> He couldn't find an apple tree.

•

What do you get when you cross
an apple with an alligator?

> An apple that takes a
> bite out of you before you
> can take a bite out of it.

How do you know a well-mannered apple tree when you meet one?

By its boughs (bows).

•

What's red and gets forty-eight miles per gallon in the city?

The economy-model apple.

•

Why are apples red?

If they were yellow they would be lemons.

•

When an apple hits a peach in the mouth, what do you call it?

A fruit punch.

•

What would you have if you crossed an apple with a goat?

Apple butter.

What would you get
if you crossed an apple
with an evergreen?

A pineapple.

•

What do you get when
you cross an apple
with a shellfish?

A crab apple.

•

What single fruit do
two apples become?

A pear (pair).

•

What food do you have
when an apple sleeps
first on its stomach and
then on its back?

An apple turnover.

What lives in apples
and is an avid reader?

A bookworm.

●

What has two hands and rings?

An alarm apple.

●

What legendary hero is
least liked by apples?

William Tell. After all,
who enjoys being shot at?

●

Which famous Norseman sailed the
Atlantic a thousand years ago?

Eric the Red Apple.

●

Who stole from the rich
and gave to the poor?

Robin Apple.

Grapes Are Great

How can you tell a California
grape from one grown in Ohio?

> By its suntan.

•

What do you get when you
cross a grape with a lion?

> A grape nobody picks on.

•

What is a raisin?

> A grape with lots of worries.

•

When should a plump
grape go on a diet?

> When it can no longer
> see its feet.

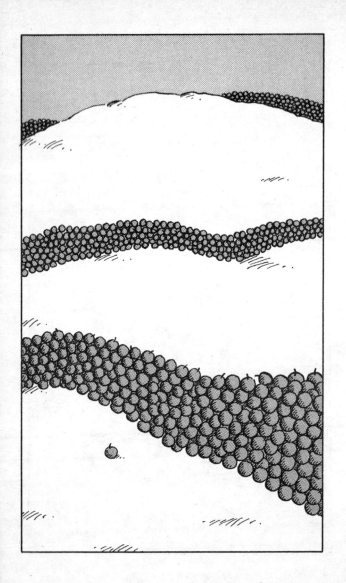

What do we call lakes
filled with grape juice?

    The Grape Lakes.

●

What is the largest thing
ever made of grapes?

    The Grape Wall of China.

●

What glows in the dark?

    A two-hundred-watt grape.

●

What was the raisin
before its diet?

    A plump grape.

●

What famous woman ruled
Russia for many years?

    Catherine the Grape.

Plum Fun

What should you do if your
pet plum becomes ill?

    Call the plumber.

●

Who cornered the market on plums?

    Little Jack Horner.

●

What do you have when
thirty-seven plums try
to go through the
door at the same time?

    Plum jam.

●

Nine plums were trapped in a
burning building. In the nick
of time, a neighbor plum brought
a ladder and saved them.
What does this prove?

    A plum in time saves nine.

What plum wrote under an alias?

Nom de Plum.

•

What is the famous novel about the
heroine who eloped with the plum?

Gone with the Plum.

•

What is the plum's favorite
Laura Ingalls Wilder story?

On the Banks of Plum Creek.

•

What do you get when you cross
a plum and a shoemaker?

A plum cobbler.

•

What is purple, has scars on
its head, and frightens people?

Frankenplum.

Why is a plum a good museum keeper?

Plum preserves.

•

How do you pick a
six-hundred-pound plum?

Very carefully.

•

What do you get if you
cross a plum and a tiger?

A purple people eater.

•

What did the plum say after
the big Christmas dinner?

"I'm plum full."

•

What is purple and hops?

A pogo plum.

•

What slogan appears on
United States coins?

E plumbus unum.

What is purple and has eight legs?

    An octoplum.

•

Why don't plums ever
get holes in themselves?

    They have pits instead.

•

Who reached the
New World in 1492?

    Christopher Plumbus.

•

Who rode a white horse
and fired silver bullets?

    The Lone Plum.

•

Who was the most dangerous
kid in the West?

    Billy the Plum.

What's purple, walks through
walls, and frightens people?

Casper the Friendly Plum.

•

Which plum was smallest?

Tom Plum.

•

Who is plump, stutters,
and loves Petunia?

Porky Plum.

•

Who are the most famous
boys in literature?

Tom Sawyer and Huck Plum.

•

Who is purple, rides a motorcycle,
and jumps trucks and buses?

Evel Plum.

Who fought for his
country in 1776?

Yankee Doodle Plum.

•

What English ruler had six wives?

Henry the Plum.

•

The world's greatest detective
lived in England, wore a deer-
stalker hat, smoked a pipe, and
was friends with Dr. Watson.
Who was he?

Sherlock Plum.

•

What Mother Goose character had
a wife but couldn't keep her?

Peter Plumkin Eater.

•

What were the authors
at the end of this page?

Plum tired.

A Peach of a Pear

What do you call twins
whose mother is a peach
and whose father is a pear?

A peach of a pair.

●

What time of year is hardest
on an overripe peach?

The fall.

●

What is a talk given
by a fuzzy fruit?

A peachy speech.

●

What is a beautiful piece of fruit?

A fair pear.

How do you tell a
peach from a 747?

> A peach's fuel tank is
> too small for it to
> cross the Atlantic
> without midair refueling.

●

Why don't peaches drive
in the great auto races?

> They are on the
> pit crew instead.

●

Why can't peaches ever
get enough to eat?

> They always have
> a pit inside.

●

Which of Poe's short stories
is most frightening to a cherry?

> "The Pit and the Pendulum."

What are deep holes in
a cherry orchard called?

Cherry pits.

●

How can you tell a pear
from an elephant?

A pear always forgets.

●

What do you get when you
cross a pear with an elephant?

A pear that never forgets.

●

Why do pears forget?

What do they have
to remember?

●

How were Humpty Dumpty and the
pear with a weak stem alike?

Both had a great fall.

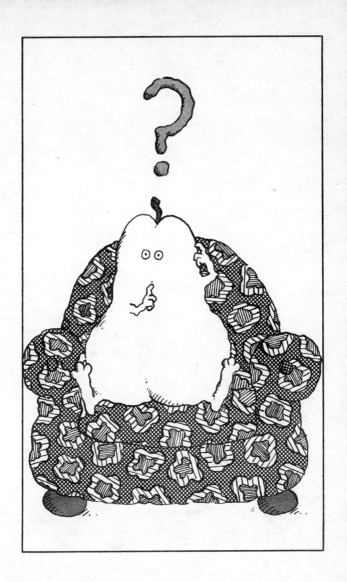

Why wouldn't the ripe peach
sit on the wall?

> It had heard what happened
> to Humpty Dumpty.

•

What is the pear's
favorite soap opera?

> "As the Pear Turns."

•

What do you call a peach that is
green and skinny at harvest time?

> A failure.

•

How do you keep a peach
from ripening in August?

> Pick it in July.

•

When does a pear
wear a yellow shirt?

> When its green one
> is in the laundry.

Knock, knock.
    Who's there?
Pear.
    Pear who?

    Pear of shoes.

●

Knock, knock.
    Who's there?
Shoes.
    Shoes who?

    Shoes me, I didn't mean
    to step on your pear.

●

Who guards our President?

    Secret Service pears.

●

What did the young lad say after
he ate a basket of ripe peaches?

    "Burp!"

●

Which spirit is found in a bottle?

    Peach brandy.

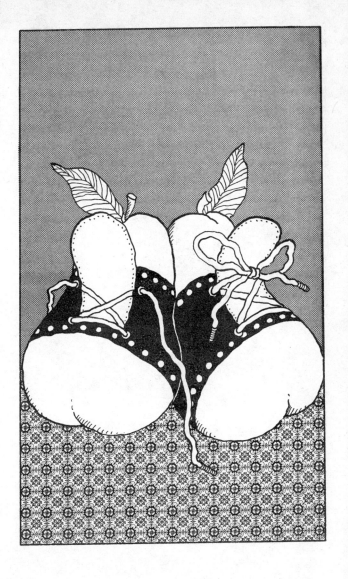

Why don't pears play basketball?

> Have you ever seen a
> pear wearing sneakers?

●

A ripe peach fell on the
farmer's head and almost
killed the poor fellow.
Why did it hurt him so badly?

> The peach was in a can.

●

Who swings through the trees
and yells like a peach?

> Tarzan of the Peaches.

●

Jill has a cherry tree eleven
years old and twelve feet tall.
How many bushels of apples
will it produce in a good year?

> None. Cherry trees
> rarely produce apples.

Citrus Fruits Have More Fun

What was the orange
doing in the palm tree?

> It had heard that
> coconuts have more fun.

●

What TV show is a favorite
with citrus fruit?

> "What's My Lime?"

●

Why don't oranges ever
play the trumpet?

> It's lemons that pucker,
> not oranges.

●

Why don't grapefruit tie
their own shoelaces?

> If you had a shape like
> a grapefruit you couldn't
> see your feet either.

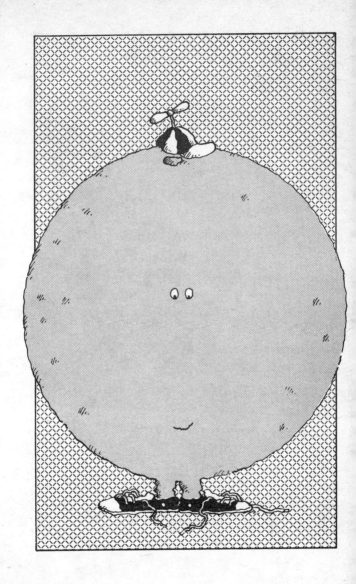

What is a ten-cent citrus fruit called?

A dime lime.

•

Why don't lemons ever
become professional fighters?

Because they are
basically yellow.

•

What do you get when you cross
a lemon with a ten-dollar bill?

Sourdough.

•

How are a lemon and
a dinosaur different?

Very few dinosaurs are yellow.

•

What's the best thing to
do for a blue orange?

Cheer it up.

What is square and green?

A lemon in disguise.

•

What is a tangerine?

An orange in an
easy-open wrapper.

•

What fruit do boys
and girls like best?

Dates.

•

How do you know that olive oil
is good for the skin?

Just think how few
wrinkled olives you see.

•

Why are grapefruit safe
from pickpockets?

Who ever saw a grapefruit
with pockets?

What's yellow and goes
bam, bam, bam, bam?

A four-door lemon.

•

What is yellow, has four doors, and
goes beep, beep, beeeeeeeeeeeeeep?

A lemon with a stuck horn.

•

Why was the grapefruit bald?

Did you ever see
one with hair?

•

What is yellow and
goes putt, putt, putt?

An outboard lemon.

•

What's huge and yellow
and says, "Fe-fi-fo-fum"?

A giant grapefruit.

What fruit leads a shocking life?

  The currant.

•

What's yellow, battery operated,
and sends radio signals?

  A shortwave lemon.

•

Why wasn't the grapefruit
a good fire fighter?

  Its helmet kept slipping off.

•

What's sour and yellow and
enforces federal laws?

  An FBI lemon.

•

What is the difference between
a lemon and a melon?

  The order in which the
  letters are written.

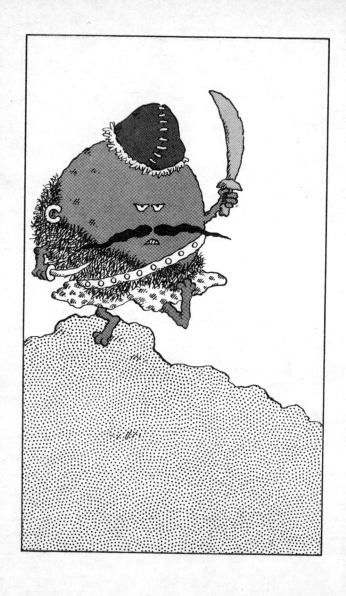

How do you make a lemon drop?

Shake the tree very hard.

•

Who was Europe's cruelest
barbarian invader?

Attila the Orange.

•

Who kept their stolen riches
in a secret cave?

Ali Baba and the
forty oranges.

•

Knock, Knock.
Who's there?
Orange.
Orange who?
Orange you glad this
is the last citrus joke!

Friends of the Jolly Green Giant

What does the government do
for endangered strawberries?

Puts them in preserves.

•

What do you have when a
thousand angry, honking strawberries
are crowded into one place?

A strawberry jam.

•

Where do you find chili beans?

At the North Pole.

•

What garden vegetable has
a nasty disposition?

A mean bean.

•

Which garden plant has eyes
but never needs glasses?

The potato.

What did the green pepper
say to the cook?

> "No more for me, please.
> I'm stuffed."

•

Who wrote our national anthem?

> Francis Scott Pea.

•

What did the little bean say
when the mother bean
asked if he had taken a nap?

> "Is one missing?"

•

Which plot of land produces
the most intelligent vegetables?

> The wiseacre.

•

What happened to the potato
that refused to work?

> It was sacked.

Why do strawberries
never grow tall?

How would it sound to have
a strawberry longcake?

•

What vegetable grows on the farmer's
foot as well as in his fields?

Corn.

•

What is the difference between a
young cornstalk and a young carrot?

The corn wants to grow up;
the carrot wants to grow down.

•

What did the tomato say after
it was run over by a truck?

"I doubt if I'd have the
guts to do that again."

•

What musical group
do potatoes hate?

The Beatles.

Two tomato plants lived in a glass greenhouse. They became angry and began throwing stones at each other. The stones broke all the windows. That night a frost came and killed both tomato plants. What lesson is to be learned from the two tomatoes?

Tomatoes who live in glass houses shouldn't throw stones.

•

Which part of the corn is in the army?

The kernel (colonel).

•

What did the strawberry say to its talkative friend?

"Thanks to your big mouth we're both in a jam."

Did you hear the story about
the world's tallest cornstalk?

Never mind, it's
over your head anyway.

●

What did the corn say
to the stuck-up scarecrow?

"You're nothing
but a stuffed shirt."

●

When did the strawberry
most need help?

When it was in a jam.

●

Why didn't the corn
get its work done?

It spent too much time
stalking around.

●

What vegetable do plumbers fix?

Leeks.

How can you tell that
strawberries are lazy?

They spend their
entire lives in beds.

•

What happened to the greenhouse
when it was enlarged to make room
for the giant asparagus stalk?

It had growing panes (pains).

•

Which vegetable pays no attention
to what is being said?

Everything corn hears goes
in one ear and out the other.

•

Why was the tomato
in such a hurry?

It wanted to
ketchup (catch up).

Getting to the Root of the Matter

A cook put 1,241 carrots into the soup broth. No one would eat the soup. What lesson is to be learned from the cook and the carrots?

Too many carrots
spoil the broth.

●

What is a well-groomed vegetable?

A neat beet.

●

What do you call a
turnip who steals?

A thief.

●

How do you tell the good carrots
from the bad ones?

The good carrots
wear white hats.

What do you call an
eight-hundred-pound turnip
with a nasty temper?

Sir!

•

Why did the carrot
color itself green?

So it could hide in
the cucumber patch.

•

Did you ever see a carrot
in a cucumber patch?

See, the disguise worked.

•

What goes
thump, swish, thump, swish?

A turnip with
one wet tennis shoe.

•

What do you call a turnip that
rides first class in a DC-10?

A passenger.

What did the exhausted vegetable say?

"Man, I'm beet" (beat).

●

Where can you find parsnips,
rutabagas, broccoli, and asparagus
no matter what time of year it is?

In the dictionary.

●

Why wouldn't the rooster
fight the angry turnip?

He was chicken.

●

Why is a turnip a better fighter
than a rooster?

The turnip isn't a chicken.

●

What goes round and round
and round and round?

A long-playing radish.

●

How do you keep a beet in suspense?

Hang it up by its toes.

What did the agent say
to the glamorous rutabaga
who was out of work?

"Don't worry. Something
will turnip soon."

•

How are a parsnip and
a stalactite alike?

They both grow down.

•

When is a sack of carrots
not a sack of carrots?

When it becomes a meal.

•

What did the turnip
say to the insects?

"You guys really bug me!"

•

Why aren't beets
good bridge players?

The cards keep slipping
out of their hands.

Heads Up

How can you tell an apple
from a head of lettuce?

> If it's red it's
> probably an apple.

●

Why didn't the little Dutch
cabbage plug the leaking dike?

> It didn't have a thumb
> to put in the hole.

●

Why wouldn't the cabbage
eat the candy that
had artificial ingredients?

> It was a health-foods nut.

●

Why did the cabbage eat a
case of fortune cookies?

> It wanted to become wealthy.

Why was the cabbage disliked
by the others in the garden?

It had a big head.

•

What did the lettuce say to
the turnip at the dull party?

"Lettuce leaf" ("Let us leave").

•

When the cabbage raced
the squash, who won?

At the end of the race
the cabbage was a head.

•

Which vegetable is the most
excitable at harvest time?

The lettuce always loses
its head during harvest.

•

What vegetable would you
get if you crossed a dog
and a blooming plant?

A cauliflower (a collie flower).

How is a rotten cabbage
like a nose?

Both smell.

•

What did the cannibalistic
cabbage say after dinner?

"I'm fed up with having
friends for dinner."

•

What do cabbages use for stockings?

Garden hose.

•

How should you tell a
two-hundred-pound cabbage
who lifts weights that
you've stolen his girl friend?

By long distance.

•

How did the cabbage
talk to the lettuce?

Head to head.

Clinging Vines

What TV show do cucumbers like best?

"Let's Make a Dill."

•

How can you find the most
attractive cucumber in the patch?

She's the one with the
most boyfriends.

•

What is orange and gets
eight miles per gallon
in town and twelve miles per
gallon on the highway?

A gas-guzzling pumpkin.

•

What turns green, amber, red,
green, amber, red, green, amber, red?

A cucumber working
as a traffic signal.

Why did the pumpkin substitute
for the football at the Super Bowl?

> He thought he would
> get a kick out of it.

•

When do cucumbers wear cleats?

> Only when they play
> on natural turf.

•

How do you harvest a watermelon that
has been crossed with a porcupine?

> Very carefully.

•

Why did Cinderella's fairy godmother
change a pumpkin into a golden coach?

> She didn't have a lemon handy.

•

A huge pumpkin rolled down a
moss-covered hillside. At the bottom
of the hill the pumpkin had no moss
clinging to it. What does that prove?

> A rolling pumpkin
> gathers no moss.

What is an
overweight pumpkin called?

A plumpkin.

●

Why do boy pumpkins
wear blue bow ties?

So you can tell them
from girl pumpkins.

●

What do you call a cucumber
who has written a book?

An author.

●

What's green and is
carried by soldiers?

A .30-caliber
automatic cucumber.

●

What is used to move money
from bank to bank?

An armored pumpkin.

When is a watermelon
most like a squash?

> When it has been
> run over by a tractor.

●

Why don't muskmelons ever
get married on short notice?

> Because they cantaloupe
> (can't elope).

●

What happens when you put 136
watermelons in your refrigerator?

> To begin with,
> the door won't close.

●

Why was the talkative cucumber
nicknamed "Track Star"?

> It was always running off
> at the mouth.

●

Why did the cucumber take
a flashlight to bed?

> It was a light sleeper.

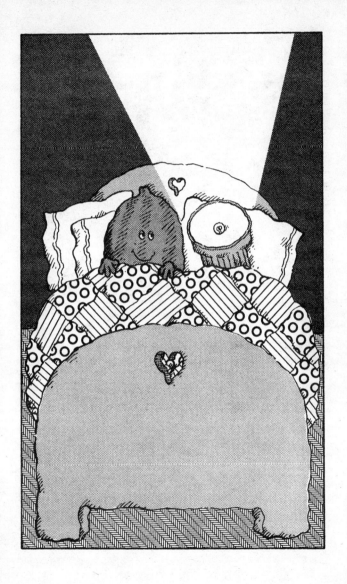

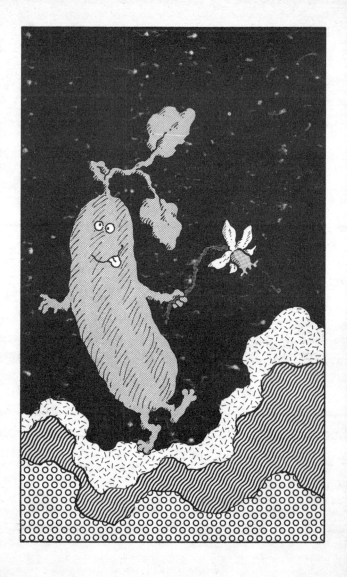

Where are pumpkins bought and sold?

On the New York
Pumpkin Exchange.

•

A farmer's watermelons were
stolen from his barn, so he
rushed out and locked the
barn door. What lesson is to
be learned from the farmer
and the watermelons?

It's useless to lock
the barn door after the
watermelons are gone.

•

Why was the cucumber
ashamed of its relatives?

They always came home
from parties pickled.

•

What flower is like a
crazy mixed-up cucumber?

A (daffodil) daffydill.

What always clings
to iron and steel?

    A magnetic cucumber.

•

Why did the police
arrest the pumpkin?

    It was involved
    in a garden plot.

•

A yellow squash married
an orange pumpkin. What
will their son be called?

    Homer.

•

Who was North America's
greatest logger?

    Paul Pumpkin.

•

What is big and orange,
lives in a Scottish lake,
is looked for constantly,
but is seldom seen?

    The Loch Ness pumpkin.

When is a watermelon most like a squash?
    When it has been run over by a tractor.

Why don't apples have teeth?
    Because they don't have any fingernails to bite.

What is the largest thing ever made of grapes?
    The Grape Wall of China.

What fruit do boys and girls like best?
    Dates.

What does a barrel of monkeys do for a laugh?
They read **The Bionic Banana**, of course!
Hundreds of nuttier-than-a-fruitcake jokes and riddles,
featuring looney lemons, mirthful melons, pesky peaches
and plums, in the fruitiest collection ever!

ISBN 0-440-90852-3